This book is dedicated to all the amazing children with Autism. Always remember, you are special, not weird.

Christina looked through the car window as Mommy drove her to school.

It was her first day. Christina just turned six-years-old, and now it was time for first grade.

I can't believe it's already time," Mommy said. Christina flapped her arms and blinked her eyes. She was so happy, and that was one of the ways she expressed it. Sometimes words were hard to speak or listen to, so Christina spoke in other ways.

Christina had Autism.

Everyone has strengths and weaknesses, every last one of us. Christina had many, many strengths, but having autism meant it was super hard to pay attention.

Sometimes NOISE would upset her, like a dog barking,

a truck's big grumbly engine, or a door slamming.

Sometimes W-O-R-D-S were hard to understand or say

And sometimes, Christina didn't want to be touched.

Everyone is different and special in their own way,"

Mommy always told Christina

Now it was time to go to first grade! The school was big, and there were we a lot of kids. Mommy asked if Christina wanted Mommy to hold her hand.

Christina nodded, which meant... yes, please!

Mommy held her hand, and they went to meet Mrs. Redding, Christina's new teacher.

"Oh, hello, Christina!" said Mrs. Redding brightly. "I'm so glad you're in our class."

Christina smiled and flapped her arms.

"I see you're very happy," Mrs. Redding said. "You know, we've had many students with autism in my class. You're going to do very well. Is it all right if I tell the other students about your autism?"

Christina turned to Mommy, who smiled.

Christina blinked, flapped, and said, "Yes!"

"Wonderful!" said Mrs. Redding

Mommy said goodbye to Christina, and soon, Christina walked to class with Mrs. Redding.

Another girl in class, Ayana, said, "Hello, Christina."
Christina didn't turn to Ayana and look at her. Instead,
she shook her head and looked at the floor.

Sometimes, Ayana," said Mrs. Redding, "Christina will find it difficult to speak. And sometimes, she may not want to touch you. But remember, it's not because she doesn't like you."

Sometimes children with autism avoid or resist physical contact. Remember: it has nothing to do with you; instead, it's about what makes Christina feel comfortable.

At lunch, Christina walked around her table ten times. Sometimes she moved her head, and sometimes she moved her arms. When she was ready, she sat down and ate her food.

"Sometimes, we need to do special things before we eat," said Mrs. Redding.

"Oh," said Ayana. "I think I understand! I like to make sure all my food is in a row before I eat."

Later, when Mrs. Redding was reading, one boy dropped a book on the floor. It made a loud noise: BOOM!

Christina began to whine, and she laid her head on her desk, covering her ears.

Sometimes," Mrs. Redding said, "loud sounds can be painful to Christina."

After story time, when Christina sat with some new friends, Mrs. Redding said it was time for finger-painting.

But Christina began to wave her arms.

"It's all right, Christina," said Mrs. Redding. "Do you not like how the paint feels on your fingertips?"

"No, sorry, Mrs. Redding," said Christina. "I don't."

Mrs. Redding smiled. "Try this."

Mrs. Redding gave Christina a paintbrush. Christina slowly wrapped her fingers around it.

She smiled and waved it around.

"That's better," she said.

Christina didn't like orange or red. Those colors made her shiver and shake, so she chose green and purple instead.

"Beautiful, Christina," Mrs. Redding said.

Sometimes the way something looks or feels—for instance, the way a book feels in Christina's hands, like the cardboard or paper, makes her feel unpleasant. To her friends, it feels normal, but to Christina, it might feel strange.

Her classmates were confused at first, but then began to help Christina, and soon everyone was comfortable.

Mrs. Redding taught the children to: be patient, always stay positive, and show love and interest.

Mommy said she'd come to pick Christina up right after Mrs. Redding told the class school was over.

And guess what?

Mommy was right at the door, waiting for Christina! Christina loves when everything goes as planned. A regular routine is important for her and makes her feel safe.

Ayana waved to Christina, who waved both arms back.

"Bye, bye," she said.

And then Christina ran to Mommy and hugged her, and she even ran in circles, flapping her arms.

"You're so happy!" said Mommy. "You must've had a great first day at school."

Christina smiled and said, "I did, Mommy! I did!"

And she couldn't wait to go back the next day.

THE END

Made in the USA
Middletown, DE
13 June 2022